This Book Belongs To:

_____

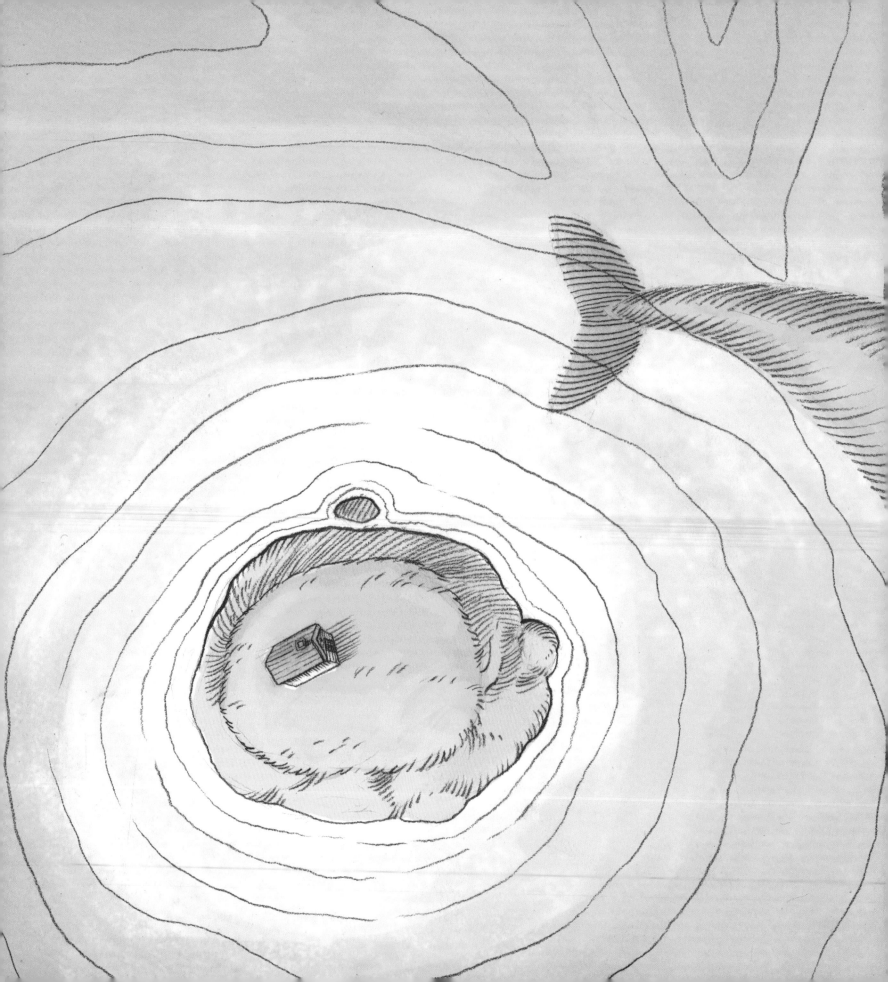

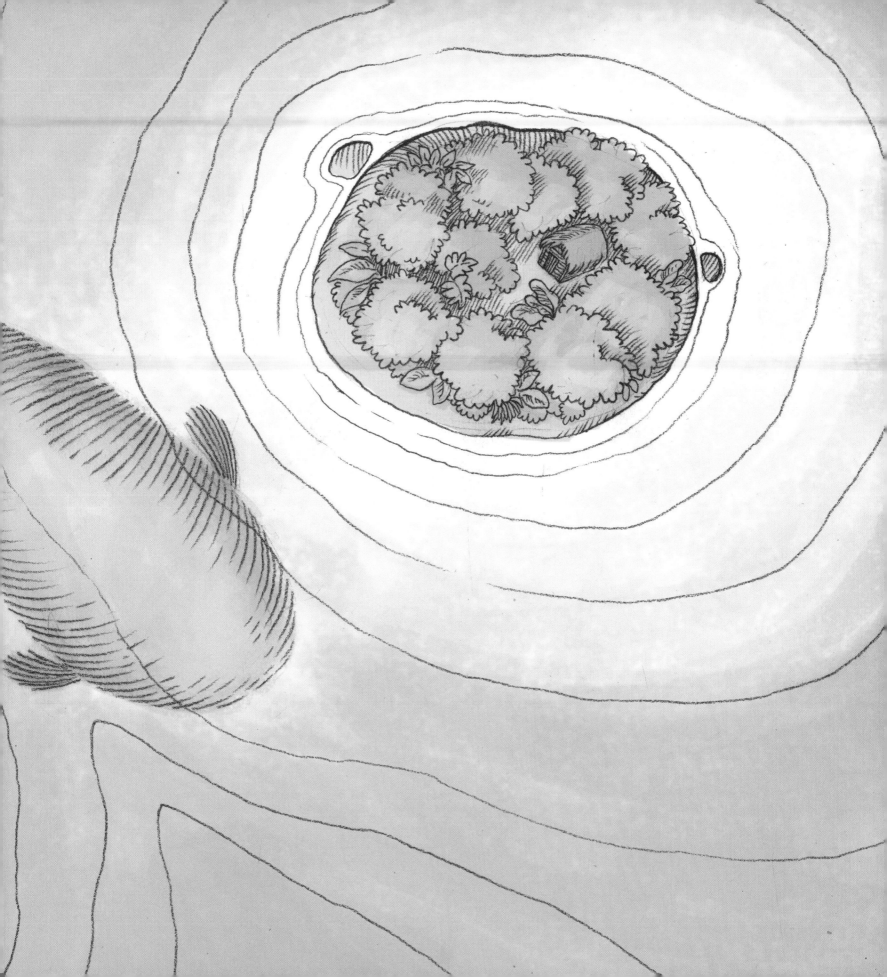

For Despina, who was on the other island

First published in Great Britain in 2016 by Andersen Press Ltd.
This paperback edition published in Great Britain in 2017 by Andersen Press Ltd.,
20 Vauxhall Bridge Road, London SW1V 2SA.
Copyright © Dan Ungureanu, 2016.
The right of Dan Ungureanu to be identified as the author and illustrator
of this work has been asserted by him in accordance with the Copyright,
Designs and Patents Act, 1988. All rights reserved.
Colour separated in Switzerland by Photolitho AG, Zürich.
Printed and bound in China.

1 3 5 7 9 10 8 6 4 2

British Library Cataloguing in Publication Data available.
ISBN 978 1 78344 535 6

dan ungureanu

Nara
and the
Island

Andersen Press

My home is so small, you can't lose anything.
At least, that's what my dad says.

But sometimes I felt like getting lost

so I would go to my secret hiding place

and look out at the other island.

Then I'd dream about how I'd get over to it.

I could make long legs and run across...

I could ask the birds to fly me there...

I could borrow Dad's bottle collection and empty the sea.

But I would have needed
a million, billion bottles.

So instead of dreaming, I always ended up feeling sad.

Or I did until today, when Dad
found my hiding place.

He says now he's fixed our boat, we can have a real adventure.

He's going to find
the Big Fish.

It's in lots of his books, but no one has ever caught it.

And if I stay close to shore,
I can explore the island
while he rows around it.

Up close, the island is bigger...

and greener and noisier and stranger.

Full of curious shapes, funny sounds and odd-looking things.

It's scary and I want to go home.
But then I meet the biggest surprise of all,
called Aran.

Aran says some of the
funny-looking things
are his best friends.

I tell him about my home, a little small and
quiet, where it's hard to find a hideaway.

He tells me about his home, so noisy and wild,
he's always trying to find a bit that's just his.

Aran has one secret place though. It's so beautiful, he's never shown it to anyone.

But maybe we could share it.

I think I'd like that.

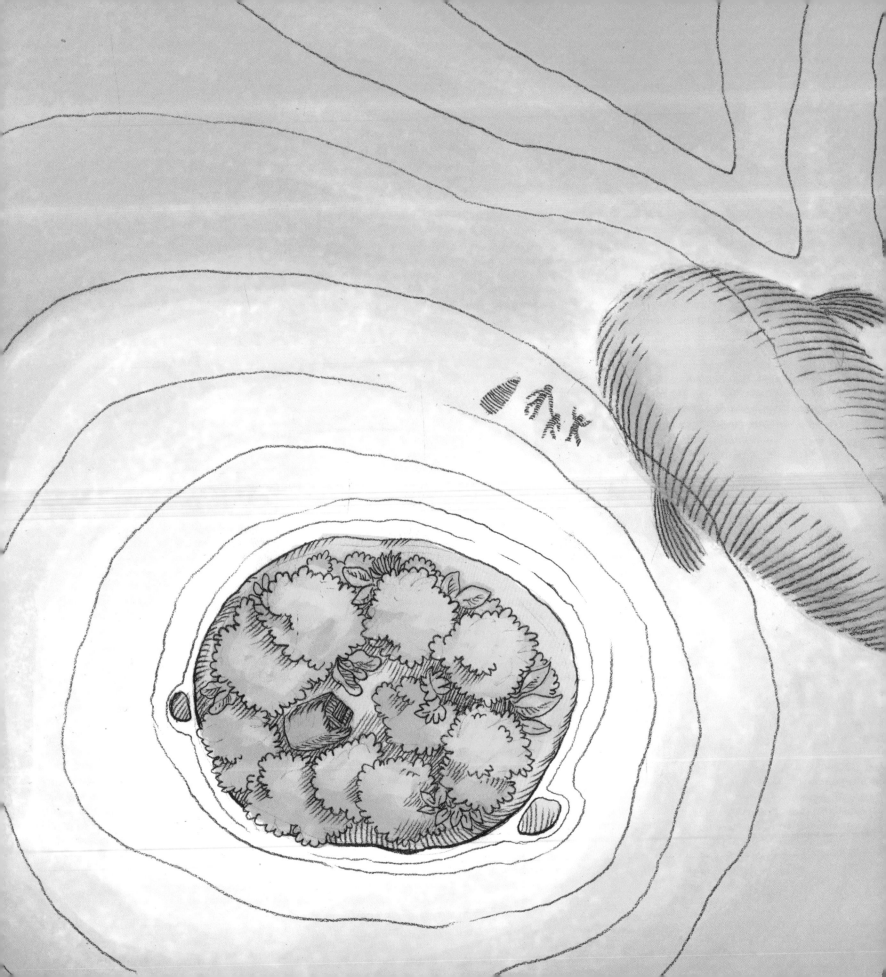